SOME SHORT
STORIES OF
LORD DUNSANY

BY

LORD DUNSANY

British Library Cataloguing-in-Publication Data
A catalogue record for this book is available from the
British Library

CONTENTS

LORD DUNSANY

Lord Dunsany was born Edward John Moreton Drax Plunkett in London in 1878. Dunsany's youth was spent in Dunsany, Ireland – his family home – and Kent. He attended school at Cheam and Eton, before entering the Royal Military Academy Sandhurst in 1896. He inherited his father's title shortly before fighting in the Second Anglo-Boer War between 1899 and 1901. Dunsany published his first book a collection of Anglo-Irish fantasy stories entitled *The Gods of Pegana*, in 1905.

Over the course of his life, Dunsany was a prolific writer, penning short stories, novels, plays, poetry, essays and autobiography. During the peak of his career he was something of a literary celebrity, spending time with authors such as W. B. Yeats and Rudyard Kipling. He published over sixty books, and his plays were highly successful; at one point, five Dunsany works were running simultaneously in New York. His most notable fantasy short stories were published between 1905 and 1919, in collections such as *The Sword of Welleran and Other Stories* (1908), *A Dreamer's Tales* (1910), *The Book of Wonder* (1912) and *Tales of Wonder* (1916). Amongst his best-regarded novels are *Don Rodriguez: Chronicles of Shadow Valley* (1922), *The King of Elfland's Daughter* (1924), and *The Charwoman's Shadow* (1926).

1

Dunsany died in old age, following an attack of appendicitis. Over the course of his writing life, he greatly influenced a wide range of authors. Arthur C. Clarke called him "one of the greatest writers of [the 20th] century," and H. P. Lovecraft described him as being "unexcelled in the sorcery of crystalline singing prose, and supreme in the creation of a gorgeous and languorous world of incandescently exotic vision."

THE MAGICIAN

LORD DUNSANY

*   *   *

It was underground. In that dank cavern down below
Belgrave Square the walls were dripping. But what was that
to the magician? It was secrecy that he needed, not dryness.
There he pondered upon the trend of events, shaped destinies
and concocted magical brews.

For the last few years the serenity of his ponderings had
been disturbed by the noise of the motor-bus; while to his
keen ears there came the earthquake-rumble, far off, of the
train in the tube, going down Sloane Street; and what he
heard of the world above his head was not to its credit.

He decided one evening over his evil pipe, down there in his dank dark chamber, that London had lived long enough, had abused its opportunities, had gone too far, in fine, with its civilization. And so he decided to wreck it.

Therefore he beckoned up his acolyte from the weedy end of the cavern, and, 'Bring me,' he said, 'the heart of the toad that dwelleth in Arabia and by the mountains of Bethany.' The acolyte slipped away by the hidden door, leaving that grim old man with his frightful pipe, and whither he went who knows but the gipsy people, or by what path he returned; but within a year he stood in the cavern again, slipping secretly in by the trap while the old man smoked, and he brought with him a little fleshy thing that rotted in a casket of pure gold.

'What is it?' the old man croaked.

'It is,' said the acolyte, 'the heart of the toad that dwelt once in Arabia and by the mountains of Bethany.'

The old man's crooked fingers closed on it, and he blessed the acolyte with his rasping voice and claw-like hand uplifted; the motor-bus rumbled above on its endless journey; far off the train shook Sloane Street.

'Come,' said the old magician, 'it is time.' And there and then they left the weedy cavern, the acolyte carrying a cauldron, gold poker and all things needful, and went abroad in the light. And very wonderful the old man looked

4

in his silks.

Their goal was the outskirts of London; the old man strode in front and the acolyte ran behind him, and there was something magical in the old man's stride alone, without his wonderful dress, the cauldron and wand, the hurrying acolyte and the small gold poker.

Little boys jeered till they caught the old man's eye. So there went on through London this strange procession of two, too swift for any to follow. Things seemed worse up there than they did in the cavern, and the further they got on their way towards London's outskirts the worse London got. 'It is time,' said the old man, 'surely.'

And so they came at last to London's edge and a small hill watching it with a mournful look. It was so mean that the acolyte longed for the cavern, dank though it was and full of terrible sayings that the old man said when he slept.

They climbed the hill and put the cauldron down, and put therein the necessary things, and lit a fire of herbs that no chemist will sell nor decent gardener grow, and stirred the cauldron with the golden poker. The magician retired a little apart and muttered, then he strode back to the cauldron and, all being ready, suddenly opened the casket and let the fleshy thing fall in to boil.

Then he made spells, *then* he flung up his arms; the fumes from the cauldron entering in at his mind he said raging things that he had not known before and runes that were dreadful (the acolyte screamed); there he cursed London from fog to loam-pit, from zenith to the abyss; motor-bus, factory, shop, parliament, people. 'Let them all perish,' he said, 'and London pass away, tram lines and bricks and pavement, the usurpers too long of the fields, let them all pass away and the wild hares come back, blackberry and briar-rose.

'Let it pass,' he said, 'pass now, pass utterly.'

In the momentary silence the old man coughed, then waited with eager eyes; and the long hum of London hummed as it always has since first the reed-huts were set up by the river, changing its note at times but always humming, louder now than it was in years gone by, but humming, night and day though its voice be cracked with age; so it hummed on.

And the old man turned round to his trembling acolyte and terribly said as he sank into the earth: 'YOU HAVE NOT BROUGHT ME THE HEART OF THE TOAD THAT DWELLETH IN ARABIA AND BY THE MOUNTAINS OF BETHANY!'

A DAY ON THE BOG

There was gentlemen in Ireland in the old days, said Mickey Tuohey, such as you very seldom see now. Severals of them there were, and all of them great gentlemen. And I'll tell you what they used to do: when they'd go out shooting grouse on the bog they'd take silver flasks with them that held as much as a quart of whiskey. A quart of whiskey in one flask. Sure, you never see anything like that nowadays. The old stock are nearly all gone, more's the pity. I mind the time when Mr Fitzcharles (the light of Heaven to him, for he is dead long ago) went out on the red bog one day, and he takes me with him to mind the dog. And the bog went right to the horizon and over the other side of it. And we walked all day, and when it got near to one o'clock, and we had a fine bag of snipe and a few grouse, he says to me, 'What about a bit of lunch, Tuohey?'

And I says to him, 'Sir, it was the very thing I was thinking myself.'

And we sits down on the heather and eats a few sandwiches, and that sort of stuff, that I had in the game-bag. And then he says to me, 'Did you happen to remember to bring my flask, Tuohey?'

Remember it! Sure I remember it to this day.

And I says, 'I did, sir.'

And I brings out the great silver flask that used to hold a quart.

'Then shall we have a little whiskey,' he says, 'to keep our throats from getting dry?'

And I had two tumblers in the game-bag, made of horn, the way that they wouldn't break. And our throats never got dry that morning. It was the best of old whiskey that Mr Fitzcharles used to have in those days, mild as milk, and did you no more harm nor milk, and a great deal more good. And Mr Fitzcharles gave me half of it for myself, and he drinks his half straight off, without taking a breath. That's the kind of grand old gentleman that he was. We sat there in the sun resting and feeling the good that the whiskey was doing us, and the red bog round us as far as the eye could see. And a leprechaun comes over the bog and he runs straight up to us, the only time in my life I ever seen a leprechaun close, though I'd often heard tell of them; a little brown lad not half the height of a man. And he stands there on a patch of bright-red moss and looks at us. And he says to us, 'You are the two grandest men ever I seen.'

And Mr Fitzcharles says to him, 'Is there anything I can do for you?'

And the leprechaun says, 'Sure, there is. Would your honour give me your soul, that I may become a mortal and go about on the dry land, and see towns and wear boots and a fine glossy hat?'

And I was terrified for the sake of Mr Fitzcharles, for he was the most generous-hearted man in the world, one of the great gentlemen, and he would never refuse anyone anything; and I was afraid that he would give up his soul and be damned. But he thinks for a moment before he answers, as a man should. And then he says to the leprechaun, 'I'm afraid I'm only a Protestant.'

'Ah, well,' says the leprechaun, 'what matter? But never mind now. Sure, I'll ask you for it some other time.'

And then I was more frightened than ever, for I was afraid he would ask me for mine. And I couldn't refuse him, if he did, in the presence of Mr Fitzcharles, on account of him being one of the most generous-hearted men in the world, as I'm just after telling you. I couldn't refuse anybody anything when I was out with him, whatever I might do at another time. So I sat there trying to look the other way. But the leprechaun hops round in front of the way I was looking, quicker nor I could turn my eyes away from him. And he says to me, 'Will you lend me your soul?'

Well, you know the way it is when anyone asks you to lend him something: it is harder to refuse nor when he asks you to give it. But the result is the same either way. And I thought for a moment or two, the same as Mr Fitzcharles had done; and then I says to him, 'I'll lend you my soul for so long as you like, if you'll give me your crock of gold.'

And, mind you, it isn't that I valued the crock of gold more nor my soul. Sure, it would be a great mistake to do that. But I knew that he'd never part with his crock. And, sure, he wouldn't. And what he says is, 'Sure, I wouldn't pay you all that for it.'

'You and your crock of gold,' I says to him. 'Sure, you've not enough in it to buy a pig, let alone a good Catholic soul.'

'Begob,' he says to me, 'I've enough in it to buy a herd of cattle, and your soul as well, and another one like it thrown in for luck. And you'll not find my crock, for I'm going to run away in the opposite direction from where it is, so as not to lead you to it.'

Well, we hunted most of the evening for that crock in the opposite direction from the one in which he had run. But after a bit I says to Mr Fitzcharles, 'Maybe he's not so simple as he appeared. What if the little devil has been telling a lie to us?'

'And so he might,' says Mrs Fitzcharles. 'I would never trust a leprechaun.'

And that was perfectly right, for there was nothing Mr Fitzcharles didn't know.

So we hunted in the other direction, the one in which he *had* run. But very soon the good that the whiskey had done us seemed to begin to run out of us, and there was no more left in the flask to keep us going; and it was like looking for a snipe, without a dog, that has fallen a long way off. Sure, the red bog has a great knack of hiding things. So we give it up. The cheek of him, saying that he wouldn't make the exchange! Ah, but those were the good days. You can't get enough for two shillings to moisten your lips now.

THE CROCK OF GOLD

I remember one day at the Billiards Club, when someone was mentioned who had been made an FRSW, and Jorkens was there. 'Oddly enough,' he said, 'I might once have been an FRSW myself, if I could have afforded it.'

'You don't become a Fellow of the Royal Society of Wiseacres for cash,' said one of us.

'I didn't say you did,' said Jorkens. 'But, if I could have afforded to have gone for it instead of going for cash, I should have had a pretty good chance of being elected. Why! A man was made a Fellow the other day, who had only discovered a new species of zebra. I had a much more curious specimen of zoology to tell them about, if I hadn't gone wandering after the cash instead. I had an opportunity for study that rarely occurs.'

'And why didn't you take it?' said Terbut.

'Because it was an opportunity,' said Jorkens. 'Does one ever take them?'

Somehow Terbut was not ready with any answer. So Jorkens continued awhile without more interruption. 'It was like this,' he said; 'in Ireland once; in Munster, near to a bog. I didn't think much of crocks of gold where rainbows end; but once when I saw one blazing upon the ground, turning the grass to an intenser green than anything you can imagine, and a hedge beyond it into purple and pink, and a leprechaun actually sitting in the middle of the patch where it touched the grass, then I could hardly doubt that there must be something in it, and that that was where he had buried his crock of gold.'

'A leprechaun,' exclaimed Terbut. 'What was it like?'

'That's what I should have studied more carefully,' said Jorkens. 'But I went instead for the crock of gold.'

'You did, did you?' said Terbut.

'I did,' said Jorkens. 'I said "Good morning" to the leprechaun. And he said "Good morning" rather sulkily. "I suppose you've buried your crock of gold there," I said.

' "It's no use denying it," said he. "But neither you nor anyone would ever find my crocks of gold if it wasn't for that damned rainbow that is always giving them away."

' "Well, I've found it," I said. "And, if the rainbow guided me here, it meant me to have it. And have it I will," I said.

' "You will not," said he.

' "I'm a bigger man than you," I said, "and finding's keeping where crocks of gold are concerned."

'For that is the custom of the country, and nobody calls it robbery to take his gold from a leprechaun. He counts no more than a political opponent. A leprechaun is mere game.

' "I'm off to get a spade," I said, "from the nearest cottage;

and I'll mark the spot with something you can't pull up."

'For I'd stuck my stick in the ground and saw him eyeing it, and I took a bearing on a couple of trees with a compass I had on my watch-chain and jotted it down on paper.

' "You'll not pull up that," I said.

'But he knew nothing about compasses.

'And then he said, "And do you know what will happen if you dig up my crock of gold?"

' "I'll have some cash to spare," I said. "That's what will happen. And it hasn't happened for a very long time."

' "You will not," he said, "and I warn you. For if you start digging for that crock of gold, the crock and the rainbow and I, and the spade itself, will all turn into dreams."

' "Dreams be damned!" I said. "I'm going to get the crock."

' "It's only two foot down," said the leprechaun; "but it will be all a dream when you get it, crock and spade and rainbow and I myself."

' "Well," I said, "that's the kind of dream I like, and I'm going to get the spade."

'There was a little white-walled cottage beyond the rainbow, with an old brown thatch on it, nearly black in the hollows, except where a patch or two of pale-green oats were growing. And I went to the door and peered in over the upper half of it, which was open, and saw a man with a long thin beard, and asked him if he would be so good as to lend me a spade. Well, of course it was an odd request, and he looked a little doubtful, and I thought it was best to tell him the truth, for he would understand a thing like that. "There are rainbows about," I said, "and I'm going to dig for a crock of gold, and I'll give you one handful if you'll lend me the spade." Of course there was no danger of his going and getting the gold himself, because the end of the rainbow looked all different from where he was, and he hadn't seen the leprechaun. He was very obliging and lent me the spade, and thanked me for the offer of the handful. I might have got him to lend the spade for less, but I was in a hurry, for fear that the leprechaun should start to dig and try to remove his gold.

' "Many's the time," the old fellow said, "that I dug for them when I was young." And then he added kindly, "Maybe you'll find it." And away I went with the spade.

'The leprechaun was still there when I got back. He hadn't had time to dig up his gold and take it away, so he had not tried. "I warned you," he said. But I began to dig. I don't know if any of you have made money in shorter time, but I got down through two feet of that soft soil in little over five minutes. And there was the crock of gold, a palebrown earthern crock with the top open, and the gold shining inside. Then for the first time I sat down to rest.

Five minutes steady digging may not seem much, and isn't much to anyone that is accustomed to it. To anyone quite unaccustomed I've known it bring on lumbago that would drop a man in a heap. It didn't do that to me, but I was glad of a moment's rest; and so I sat down with my feet in the hole I had dug, one on each side of the neck of the crock of gold, and the rainbow glittering in my face. The little golden discs were shining between my feet, and I looked up at the leprechaun. "Well, there it is," I said. And all of a sudden I saw him beginning to fade. I couldn't believe it possible. I looked beyond him, and the rainbow was fading too! That startled me, and I looked hurriedly back at the crock. And that also Was fading! Back I looked at the leprechaun, and he was nearly gone. "What did I tell you?" he cried out shrilly, and wholly disappeared. And then the crock went, and the rainbow, and the hole I had dug, and, even as he had said, the spade in my hand.

'All this while the echo of his last remark was floating over the fields, going down to the heather, and was taken up by a curlew that was flying over the bog. And the thought came to me, How on earth was I to explain to the man from whom I had borrowed the spade? Well, there was no sign left of crock, hole, rainbow or leprechaun, and so there was nothing to wait for, and I hurried back to the old white cottage to apologise and explain. And there was the man with the long, thin beard, indoors where I saw him last, and I leaned in through the door and began at once to apologise. "Ah, sure I never lent you a spade," he said, in those very words. I tried once more, but he still stuck to his point. And then I saw that the spade had gone with the crock so utterly into dreamland, that in this earth it had no existence, either at that time or ever. You see what I mean?'

At first it was not clear to me, or indeed to any of us. No one spoke, except to the waiter; and soon a scene unusual at the Billiards Club might have been observed, a group of members round Jorkens, each with a whiskey-and-soda, while Jorkens had none. With a moment or two for refreshment, and one or two for reflection, it soon became clear enough, and I think we saw what he meant.

THE END OF THE RAINBOW

There was a conference only two days ago in my sitting-room between two gentlemen that were members of the government of this State, though I doubt if really they were anything more than the members' secretaries; and in any case we decided nothing, and I only mention it for the sake of a curious comparison, which is that the memory of the details of that conference is less vivid in my mind today than the things that I heard and saw on a morning fifty-two years ago when I drove over to see Marlin, hoping that, after all, Dr Rory may have been wrong. I went to Clonrue first, to see the doctor, impatient for some better news than what he had given me only the day before, and I even got it, for he had seen Marlin again, later that day. 'He's walking about a good deal,' he said.

'Then he'll live longer than you thought?' I asked.

'Ah, I think he will,' said the doctor.

And from that I tried to get him to say that perhaps he was wrong after all, and that Marlin would yet recover. What he said I cannot remember. But what does it matter? I was only asking him to echo my hopes. Dr Rory's words could not turn Fate back to walk the way that I wished. Yet neither he nor I ever guessed the end of Marlin.

'What way are you going?' he said to me then.

'There's only one way,' I answered.

'Ah, but you can't get down the bohereen,' he told me.

'Can't get down the bohereen?' said I.

'No,' said Dr Rory, 'they are making a road along it.'

'A road?' I exclaimed.

'Yes,' said the doctor.

'What ever for?' I asked.

'The Peat Development (Ireland) Syndicate,' he replied.

Then it was true. What had almost seemed like ravings, when Mrs Marlin told me, was mere accurate information. They were going to spoil the bog.

'But did my father ever give them leave?' I asked, clinging to a last hope, for it was not like him to allow syndicates and such things from towns to make a mess of the countryside.

'They bought an option for fifty pounds,' said the doctor. 'And now they've taken it up. You'll get a rent from them.'

'I don't want their rent,' I said. For it seemed like selling Ireland piecemeal, if they were going to cut the bog away. One did not feel like that about the turf-cutters, who all through the spring and summer had their long harvest of peat, that brought the benignant influence of the bog to a hundred hearths, and that filled the air all round the little villages with the odour that hangs in no other air that I know. Indeed the very land on which the Marlins' house was standing had been once about twenty feet higher, and had been brought to that level by ages of harvests of peat, or turf as we call it. And the land that was left was still Ireland. But now it was to be cumbered with wheels and rails and machinery, and all the unnatural things that the factory was even then giving the world, as the cities began to open that terrible box of Pandora.

'Why did my father do it?' I asked.

'He only sold them the option,' said the doctor. 'He never thought they'd come here with their nonsense. And fifty pounds is fifty pounds.'

'What are they going to do?' I enquired.

'Compress the turf by machinery and sell it as coal,' he answered.

'What nonsense,' I exclaimed.

'Of course it is,' he replied. 'But there's a lot of money to be made out of a company. And when it's got an address beside a bog, and is actually working there, it will look much more real to investors than when it's only in a prospectus. Not that it doesn't catch some of them even then.'

'I wish my father hadn't done it,' I said. But that was no use.

'They'll be broke in a few years,' said the doctor.

In a few years: that seemed terribly long to a boy.

'They'll ruin the bog,' I said. 'Can no one stop them?'

'I'm afraid not,' he answered.

It seemed so wrong that all that wonderful land, so beautiful and so free, should be brought under the thraldom of business by a city so far away, that my thoughts in their desperation turned strangely to Mrs Marlin.

'Could Mrs Marlin do anything?' I asked.

'I'm afraid not,' he said.

'Couldn't she lay a curse on them?' I continued.

'She might curse their souls a bit,' said the doctor reflectively, 'but they'd think more of business.'

In despair I left him then, and went on to see Marlin.

'We'll go by the other road,' I said to Ryan. 'They're spoiling the bohereen.'

And Ryan muttered something, as though he were cursing the Peat Development Company, but with an amateur's ill-trained curses; not like Mrs Marlin. So down the road we went, the other road from Clonrue. And, if it is not too late, why does not some museum preserve a few yards of an old road, as it used to be before even bicycles came to cover it with their thin tracks? It's clear enough in my memory, with its wandering wheel-tracks, its pale-grey stone bright in the sunlight, and the cracks that ran through it everywhere from its unstable foundation, as soon as it neared the bog; but when I and my memory are gone and all my generation, who will remember those roads? I suppose it will not matter. They will lie sleeping, deep under tarmac, those old white roads, like the stratum of a lost era for which nobody cares. But who cares aught for the past? That pin-point of light called The Present, dancing through endless night, is all that any man cares for.

So we drove down the other road, and along the side of the bog; and the little cracks were running among the wheel-tracks as though the bog had often whispered a warning, telling that he was amongst the ancient powers, of which the earthquake was one, and that he suffered roads as all these powers suffer the things of man, which is grudgingly and for a while. And half a mile or so from the Marlins' cottage, at the nearest point to which this road came to them, I got out of the trap. My walk lay over the level land from which the bog had receded, or rather from which it had been pushed back by man: on my left, all the way as I went, the cliff of the bog's edge stood like a wave of a threatening tide, dark and long and immanent. Square pools of sombre deep water lay here and there under the cliff, with a green slime floating in most of them, and the green slime teeming with tadpoles. I sat down by the brink of one of these pools and looked at it, for the sheer joy of being home again. I looked and saw little beetles navigating the dark water like bright pellets of lead, and rather seeming to be running than swimming. Then an insect with four legs skipped hurriedly over the surface, going from island to island of scarlet grass, and a skylark came by singing. Above me in the mosses beyond the top of the bog's sheer edge the curlews were nesting, their spring call ringing over the pools and the heather. Beside me a patch of peat was touched with green as though it had gone mouldy, and up from it went a little forest of buds, each on its slender stalk, for spring had come to the moss as well as the curlews. In amongst the soft moss grew what looked like large leaves, but so fungoid was their appearance that it was hard to say whether they belonged to the moss, or were even vegetable at all: rather they seemed to haunt the boundary of the vegetable kingdom as ghosts haunt the boundary of man's. Strangely ill-assorted were those gross leaves and the fairy-like slenderness of the stalks. I could have sat there long, watching the activity of the two kinds of insect that scurried over that water, or looking at the history of the ages in the coloured layers of the peat, which is always written wherever an edge of Earth is exposed, if only one can read it; and all the while the skylark sang on. I could have sat there idly all day in deep content, only that an anxiety thrilled through my content, and drove me on, urging me to hasten to hear the worst about Marlin. And so I walked on, under the bog's edge, with peaty soil underfoot, on which sometimes rushes grew, now all in flower, and sometimes heather, young and very green, and sometimes, almost timidly, the grass; for the grass came mostly along the tracks of the turf-carts, and where the earth was most trodden, and by little bridges across tiny streams, as though only in the immediate presence of man could it dare to usurp that land where the bog so recently reigned. And all the way as I went over that quiet land there went beside me a chronicle of the ancient shudders of Earth, old angers that had stirred and troubled the bog; for the long layers, tawny and sable, ochre, umber and orange, that were the ruins of long-decayed heather and bygone moss, went in waves all the way, sometimes heaving up into hills, the mark of some age-old uprising, sometimes cracked by clefts that sundered them twenty feet down, as though they still threatened the levels so lately stolen by man. And even that land that man had won for himself faintly shook as I trod it, making the threat of the bog all the more ominous. I passed innumerable little ditches, dug to run off the water that came down from the bog, so that the things of man might grow there and not the things of the wild. And over all of them were little bridges for the turf-carts to cross with their donkeys, for a man on foot could step over the ditches anywhere; trunks of small trees heaped over with peat and sods; but the trunks were all rotting away, so that only a prophet could tell whether man would hold that land, or whether the damp and the south-west wind and the bog would one day claim their own again.

Presently I came on turf-cutters at their work, digging out

of the brown face of the soft cliff their foot-long sections of peat, four or five inches thick and wide, with an implement that seemed a blend between a spade and a spear. I don't suppose that has altered since I was living in Ireland, nor for some centuries before that. And another thing that can scarcely ever have altered is the little turf-cart in which the pieces of fresh wet peat are drawn away by donkeys, for it has the air of having been there for ever, and I do not see what it can ever have altered from, for it is so simply primitive that it must have been nearly the first. The superstructure was like that of the wheel-barrow and little larger, but it was the wheels that had been left behind by receding ages from man's very earliest effort at drawing loads. These were merely two trunks of trees, hollowed a little where the axles should be and leaving a pair of crude wheels at the ends. An iron bar ran through the core of each trunk, connecting it to the cart, and on these the trunks revolved. Two donkeys dragged the little load away to be stacked and to dry in the spring weather, with a little heather on top to keep off the rain. In those stacks the long, brick-like pieces of chocolate-coloured turf would dry to pale ochre and be carried to the cottages to take their part in the struggle against the next winter. Two men with long black hair were working the face of the bank as I came by, cutting in level lines, as though they were taking bricks layer by layer off a wall; so that when they had come to the blacker layers underneath, and had gone as low as they could and met the water, the edge of the bog would have receded along the width of their working a distance of four inches. We greeted each other as I passed, and I went on over grass and bare peat and rushes, and over the little bridges, till I saw far off the willows that grew near the Marlins' house, shining like sunlight coming through greenish smoke. I saw the willows that I knew so well, now glorying in the spring, but I saw with a pang light flashing on roofs that were strange to me: mean buildings had come already, with the swiftness of an encampment, to that land that had always seemed to me as enchanted as any land can be. And what would come of that enchantment now? So elusive a thing, among that cluster of huts, could never survive the noise, the ugliness, the ridicule and the greed. I felt sick at heart at the sight of them; and in my despair I knew nothing that could protect the ancient wildness that was such a rest and a solace to any cares that one brought to it from the world; and, feeling helpless myself, I placed no confidence in any help that could come from Mrs Marlin.

* * *

When I saw the willows shining I hurried on, for anxiety drove me on over the little bridges to hear the news of Marlin. The curlews uttered their curious cry on my left, beyond the wavy strata, while above me a skylark sang on and on and on; and, amongst all the cries of the birds and the gleam of the willows, my melancholy deepened, standing out all the blacker against the splendour of spring.

And then I saw Mrs Marlin, far off, in her garden. She was not hurrying, she was not wailing; and I knew how grief would have racked that dark woman, giving a wild movement to her strides and a certain terror to every line of her. Or if I did not know to what fury grief would have urged her spirit, I saw at least, and even at that distance, that no great passion was driving her; although later, when I came nearer, I saw often a quick uneasy turn of her head towards the new huts and the dam that was building across the stream, as though a malevolence smouldered in her, or she rested from recently cursing; but at least Marlin was not dying; and, suddenly relieved of that fear, I walked towards her with all my anxieties gone.

'How is Marlin?' I asked, when I got within call of her.

'He's all right, sir,' she said.

I came a few paces nearer.

'I am delighted to hear that,' I said to her. 'The doctor gave a very bad account of him.'

And she laughed at that, with rather a sly look.

'Ah, what does he know?' she said.

'Where is he?' I asked.

'Ah, he's gone,' she replied.

27

'But Marlin, I mean,' said I.

'Aye. Sure, he's gone,' she answered.

'Gone?' I said. 'Where?'

'Over the bog,' she said.

'But what way?' I asked.

'A rainbow showed him,' she said.

'A rainbow?' I muttered.

And she went to the door and opened it for me, and we went in. And she offered me a chair before her great fireplace and sat down a chair herself and gazed into the red embers of the turf, which never break into flame. And then she said: 'He was very ill. Ill as the doctor said. But, sure, what does he know of anything, only of the affairs of that world?' And she pointed away from the bog.

'He was lying there in his bed yesterday evening, ill as the doctor said, and I was trying to get him to take some medicine, when he turned to me and says: "Mother, I must go. For if I stop any longer I'll be dying. And I'll not die in this earth." And I says to him: "Ireland's a good enough land for any man to die in." And he says: "Not when it's Hell you'd have to go to; and it's where I'd go from here." And at that he rises up from his bed and puts on his boots, and gives one look round at the cottage. Then he gives me a kiss and sets off, and there was a rainbow shining. And no sooner had he climbed up by the bank of turf and set his foot on the bog, but the rainbow begins to go further and further off. And he follows it all the way to the everlasting morning.'

I don't exactly know what she meant by that, but she pointed through a window as she spoke, in the direction in which the sun usually brightened far patches of water, away by the bog's horizon, all the morning; the direction in which so often I had seen Martin's eyes stray.

'But how far did he go?' I asked.

'To Tir-nan-Og,' she said.

'But how did he know the way?' said I.

'The rainbow showed him,' she answered.

What had happened to Marlin? I wondered. Where had he gone?

'How far did you see him?' I asked.

'Away and away,' she said. 'And the rainbow before him.'

'But he couldn't walk out of your sight,' I said. 'A sick man couldn't have done it.'

But still she pointed away to the far horizon, where the water shone and no hills bounded the bog.

'The night came on,' she said, 'after the rainbow left him.'

Her words frightened me. You can't walk the bog out there in the night; or it is very nearly impossible.

'You should have called him back,' I said.

'Call back a rainbow!' she exclaimed, with a gust

of laughter.

'No, Marlin,' I explained.

'Nor him, either,' she said. 'They were both of them going away to the glory of Tir-nan-Og, the rainbow from the dark world and the coming of night, and my son from damnation. Little they know the rainbow from his few visits to these fields, little they know it that have not seen it glorying in its home, entwined with the apple-blossom of the Land of the Young; and little they know of a man till they have seen him in the splendour of his youth among the everlastingly youthful in the orchards of Tir-nan-Og.'

For a moment I feared she would try to go after him, and drown herself, thinking she could not go very far in safety, at her age, over the bog.

'You're not going, too?' I asked.

'I'll never see him there,' she said. 'God knows I'll never see him there, having stayed on Earth too long, till my feet are slow with its weeds and my soul with its cares. Though I'll say nothing harsh against Earth, for the sake of Ireland. And I have one thing more to do upon Earth yet. For I have to speak with the powers of bog and storm and night, and to learn their will with the men that are harming the heather.'

'Show me the way he went,' I said, and got up from the chair; for I felt sure that a man as sick as he was could never have walked far over the bog. And she rose and came with me out of the door and we walked to the bog's edge, I impatient to find Marlin and trying to hurry her, she without any anxieties and only concerned with her reflections, which she uttered as we went.

'It's by the blessing of God,' she said, 'that mothers never see their sons grow old; bent and wrinkled and haggard. It's the blessing of God. And they should not see them die. A few days more and Tommy would have died, there in his bed beside me; and no art of mine could have hindered it; for I have no power against the splendour of death. But he rose and walked away out of the world, where age cannot overtake him, and where death is only known from idle stories told in the orchards by those that are young for ever, for the sake of the touch of sadness that gives a savour to their immortal joy. Weakness and wrinkles and dying, they are the way of this world, and the shadow of damnation creeping nearer. But he has walked away from the world and away from the shadow.'

All the while I was trying to hurry her, picturing Marlin lying a mile away out in the bog, for I feared he could scarce have got further; and how would a sick man fare, out there all night?

'Was there any frost?' I asked her; for we still had a touch of frost sometimes at night, and she was nearer to these things than I in our large house.

But she only answered: 'Aye, the world's cold,' and gazed away before her with happy eyes as though she went to her son's wedding.

'Hurry,' I said, for she would not quicken her pace. 'Or we'll find him dead.'

'Ah, no,' she said. 'He would not wait for death. And why would he, with damnation prepared for him by those that are jealous of the land of the morning?'

I don't know whom she meant; and, God knows, these are no words of mine, but only hers still haunting my memory, where I fear they should not be, and would not be if I could banish them.

And so we came to the steep edge of the bog and she climbed agilely up, and I after her; and for a while we walked in silence over the rushes. The moss lay grey all round us, crisp as a dry sponge, while we stepped on the heather and rushes, the heather all covered with dead grey buds, the rushes a pale sandy colour. I had never walked the bog in the spring before, and was surprised at the greyness of it. But some bright mosses remained, scarlet and brilliant green; and along the edge of the bog under the hills lay a slender ribbon of gorse, and the fields flashed bright above it, so that the bog lay like a dull stone set in gold, with a row of emeralds round the golden ring. A snipe got up brown, and turned, and flashed white in turning. A curlew rose and sped away down the sky with swift beats of his long wings and loud outcry, giving the news, 'Man, Man,' to all whose peace was endangered by our approach, and a skylark shot up and sang, and stayed above us, singing. The pools that in the winter lay between the islands of heather, and that Marlin used to tell me were bottomless, were most of them grey slime now, topped with a crust that looked as if it might almost bear one. We knew the way to go; the way that I had so often seen Marlin's eyes gazing, the way that Mrs Marlin said straight out was the way to Tir-nan-Og: I could see the water flashing over there, though the grey moss was dry about us. The fear that I had had that Mrs Marlin would come to harm in the bog I had now entirely forgotten, for she stepped from tussock to tussock surely and firmly, with a stride that seemed to know the bog too well to falter even with age. We came, with the skylark still singing, to pools that were partly water and partly luxuriant moss: strange grasses leaned along them and burst into flower. More and more pools them we met, and less grey moss, and presently the wide lakes lay before us, to which Marlin had looked so often. I stood on a hummock of heather and stared ahead, then looked at Mrs Marlin. There was nothing but water and rushes and moss before us. We were as far as a sick man could have walked, apart from the danger and difficulty of all that lay ahead. If Marlin had come this way there was no hope for him.

'You are sure he went this way?' I asked, and knew that the question was hopeless even as I asked it.

Her face all lighted up, looking glad and young, and with shining eyes she gazed over the desolate water, and said: 'Aye, he went this way, this way; away from the world and the shadow cast by damnation, black as tar on the cities. Aye, he went this way.'

And then I knew that Marlin shared with the Pharaohs that strange eternity of the body that only Egypt and the Irish bog can give. Centuries hence, when we are all mouldered away, some turf-cutter will find Marlin there and will look on a face and a figure untouched by all those years, even as though the body had obeyed the dream after all.

*   *   *

Then I brought Mrs Marlin back from the bog, thinking she had gone far enough, and knowing that the part of it to which we had come was dangerous walking even for a young man. For these were the waters that Marlin called 'the sumach,' or some such word that I do not know how to spell, a mass of stored rains that grew heavier every year, till it flooded in under the roots of whatever growth gave a foothold, and floated the light surface of mosses and peat, till everything trembled round one as one walked: one called it the shaky bog, the most dangerous of all the kinds of bog that one walks. These waters were the source of the stream that ran past the Marlins' house; but, as more rain came with the storms than left with the stream, the whole weight of the bog was increasing.

'We must get all the men we can find, and search the bog for him,' I said, when I got her back to the safe grey moss and the heather. And at that she laughed with peals of her strange wild laughter.

'Aye, search the world for him,' she said. 'But he will not be there. And it's not the world that wants him, but Hell. And Hell will not have him either. It's the orchards of Tir-nan-Og that have him now, with the morning dripping from their branches in everlasting light, golden and slow, like honey. Aye, and the evening too, and both together; for Time that troubles us here comes not to those gleaming shores. Age, desolation and dying; that's the way of these fields; and not one wrinkle, nor sigh, nor one white hair, ever came to Tir-nan-Og.'

'We must look for him,' I said. For it was a duty to do all that one could, even if the search seemed hopeless; and I did not wish her words to turn me away from it, as I feared that they soon would.

'Aye, search for ever,' she said, 'and you'll never see him. But I shall see him often.'

'Where?' I said.

'Where would it be,' she answered, 'but about his mother's house and over the heather that he knew as a child, and on mosses by pools where he played? Where else would he go when he comes from Tir-nan-Og, and the jack-o'-lanterns come riding the storm through the darkness, and go dancing over the bog?'

'How will he come?' I asked.

'On the west wind,' she answered.

'We must search for him,' I said, sticking to my point, which it seemed harder and harder to do.

'Aye, search,' she said, and went off again into peals of her wild laughter, which rang far over the bog and frightened the curlews.

'How could he get to Tir-nan-Og?' I asked. For if there was any chance of finding him, it would have to be done quickly, and she would not see that it was serious at all. I spoke to her all the more impatiently for the fear that I soon should believe her, and do nothing at all. And one ought to do something.

'He'd go by the way of the bog till he came to the sea,' she said. 'Didn't he know the way well?'

'And then?' I asked.

'There'll be a boat there, lifting and dropping with the lap of the tide,' she said; 'and eight queens to row it; queens that have turned from Heaven, and yet slipped away from damnation. Hell has not their souls, nor the earth their dust.'

'How could he know they'd be there?' I asked her.

'How could he know?' she said. 'I told him.'

But that made things no clearer. Then she gazed away over the bog and went on talking: ' "Hell would have me, mother," he said, "if I stay here." And when I saw he was bent on leaving the world, I said I'd help him; for he knew the way over the bog to the shore, but he'd never been on the sea. And I went one stormy night to the bog, when the wind was in the West and all the people of Tir-nan-Og were riding upon the storm, and by the edge of the water where they were flashing and admiring their heathen beauty, I called out to them: "Ancient People, there's a man that would share your everlasting glory; and Hell wants him, because he has turned his face to the West. How shall he go to find you?"

'And with tiny voices they answered me through the storm, voices shriller than the cry of the snipe and small as the song of the robin, they whose voices rang once from hill to hill over Ireland; and they said: "To the sea, to the sea."

' "And then?" I said, "Oh ancient and glorious people?"

' "What would you have of us?" they asked.

'And I lured them nearer, by a power I have, and said to them: "By that power, I need your help over the sea."

'And they said to me: "When will he come?"

'And I answered: "One of these days," which is the only time we know with the future, and all we ever will know, till it is dated and mapped as is should be.

'And they repeated one to another, with their small voices, "One of these days," till the message passed out of hearing. And I made my compact with them out there on the bog, swearing by turf and heather, as they swore by blossom and twilight. For a danger threatened the bog and I swore to guard it, and they swore to carry Tommy over the water and bring him to Tir-nan-Og. Eight fair girls, they said, that were queens of old in Ireland, would bring him over the water, waiting for him where the bog ran down to the shore, upon the day that I said. And Tommy would know them, apart from their beauty and apart from their crowns of gold, by the light that would be gleaming along the sides of the boat; for the boat would be made from the bark of birches growing in Tir-nan-Og, and the twilight that shone on them in the Land of the Young would be shining upon them still. And whether it was night in the world, or whether noon or morning, the twilight of Tir-nan-Og would be shining upon that birch-bark.'

I tried to picture a boat glowing gently in twilight while it was noon all round, with the sun bright on the water; or, more wonderful still, the birch-bark iridescent in the soft light of the gloaming, while all around was night. But thinking of this only drifted me from my purpose, which was to find a number of men and search the heather for Marlin. I was in two minds; one was the mind that listened to Mrs Marlin telling of Tir-nan-Og, of which I had already learned so much from her son; the other, a more disciplined mind, told me that the bog must be searched for Marlin whether there seemed any hope of finding him there or not. The more useless this appeared the more I clung to it, lest Mrs Marlin should lure me to forget it altogether, and a duty remain undone.

'We must search for him,' I repeated.

'Aye, search,' she said indulgently, as though the search were some trivial rite that custom idly bound me to. And I think she knew from the tone of my voice that I somehow had not my heart in it. 'Would they fail me?' she went on. 'Never.'

And I saw from her far gaze westwards, and the light in her eyes, that she was thinking of those eight queens.

We came to the bog's edge, where deep fissures ran down out of sight, as though the vast weight of the bog were too much for the banks that bounded it; and from that high edge I looked over the land lying round Marlin's cottage that had always seemed so magical to me, the land over which the old willows brooded in winter and were like an enchantment in spring, and I could have wept at what I saw. And what I saw is well enough known: I need hardly describe it: a large number of small houses meanly built, and all exactly the same, denying any difference between the tastes of one man and another, nor caring anything for any man's taste, nor expressing any feeling or preference of builder or owner. It was as though men without any passions had built them all for the dead.

They were barely finished, but men were already living in some of them, and work had already started on building the dam and putting in the wheel that was to be turned by the water and which would set the machinery clanking in the ugly house they were building. The world is full of such things, little need to describe them; the only concern that this story has with them is to tell that they came down dark upon that spot to which first my memories went whenever I was far from Ireland, racing there quicker than homing pigeons, or bees going back to the hive. And not only had they spoiled the magic that lay over all that land, deep as mists in the autumn, but they were there for the purpose of cutting the bog away; not as the turf-cutters take it, with imperceptible harvests, slowly, as years go by, a few yards in each generation, but working it out as miners work out a stratum of coal.

It was to these men that I now appealed, calling out to them from the high edge of the bog and telling them that a man was lost out there in the heather. They came at once, and I soon had about thirty of them, some of them English and some the men of Clonrue. 'Begob,' said one of the latter to me, 'if you set Englishmen walking the bog it's soon a hundred men that we'll have to look for, and not only one.' But oddly enough it was the Englishmen that took charge as soon as we started off, though they got very wet over it.

'We'll find your son for you, mam,' said one of them. 'Don't you worry.'

But she looked fiercely at him and only answered: 'Do you know the way to World's End?'

'I expect we could find it, mam,' was all he said to her.

Her eyes were blazing, and then she burst into laughter. 'And you'll only be half-way to him then,' she said.

Then we all spread out to about half a mile and walked in the direction of the deep part of the bog, from which Mrs Marlin and I had just returned, and heard her laughter still ringing in mockery of the thirty men that were trying to find her son.

We went back over the grey moss, about twenty-five yards apart, the bog-cotton flowering round us, a bright patch at the tips of the rushes, the skylark high above us singing triumphantly on.

'It's got on her mind a bit,' said one of the men, as Mrs Marlin's laughter rang out behind us.

'I'm afraid it has,' I said. For I could not explain Mrs Marlin to an Englishman.

'We'll find him all right, sir,' he said.

But he only saw that the heather was not high enough to hide anyone lying there from a searcher passing within twelve yards: he did not know the deeps of an Irish bog.

'Don't step on the bright mosses,' I said.

We went on till Mrs Marlin's laughter faded from hearing, and the only wild cries we heard were the cries of the curlews.

When I came again to that waste of water and moss, where trembling waves ran through the bog from every footstep, the line of men drew in from either side to the edges of that morass, each man seeming drawn towards it without anyone saying a word; and we all looked over the water and brilliant mosses in silence. I realised then that in bringing these thirty men over the bog I had done a conventional duty in which there was no meaning whatever.

We turned round and each man took a different line to the one by which he had come, so as to cover more ground on the way back, but nobody searched any more. I knew that they were not searching, but said no word to them, for my thoughts were in Tir-nan-Og.

AN UNLIKELY HAUL

There is a certain attitude taken by some at the Billiards Club towards my friend Jorkens, which I hope has not spread beyond its walls. If I were to express that attitude in a single word, the word would be Doubt. Whether any who have read some of the tales that I have recorded from time to time as I heard them from Jorkens may have felt any doubts of them I do not know, but I set down this tale not entirely for any slight interest it may possess for those interested in wells and the various objects their waters may be sometimes found to contain; but I more particularly record it because

I know the tale to be true, being acquainted with one of the men to whom it occurred, and able thereby to check Jorkens' veracity, who was there as a chance onlooker, but a perfectly accurate one.

'I was taking a walk in India,' Jorkens began.

'What for?' asked Terbut.

'To get away from the flies,' said Jorkens.

'How far did you have to go to do that?' asked Terbut.

'Three thousand miles,' said Jorkens. 'But why not start? In fact I felt I couldn't delay any longer. Perhaps you don't know those flies?'

Terbut shook his head rather impatiently; for we all knew, and Jorkens better than most of us, that Terbut had never travelled.

'Well,' Jorkens continued, 'I was walking over a plain with a good deal of grass on it, and it was hot enough to kill more than grass, and there was nothing to see on it except a horse grazing, if nibbling that withered stuff can be so described; and he was grazing with a bit in his mouth and a saddle on his back. And then I came suddenly on a well. A rather thick patch of grass hid it entirely, until I was right on top of it. And when I did get there I saw a little flight of steps, cut out of the dry mud of which all that part of the world seems to be made, going down to the well. And on one of the lower steps a man was seated, holding a rod. I never saw him till I stood at the top step, and he didn't see me even then, being so intent on the water.

' "Fishing?" ' I said.

' "It's a spear," ' he answered, and sat there patiently for a few more seconds, leaning over the water not looking at me, then made a jab. There was some commotion in the well, in fact more noise than I ever heard in any well before, and then he made another jab; and this time, above the noise of the threshing of water, I clearly heard a pig squeal.

' "Have you got a pig in the well?" ' I asked.

' "Sounds like it," ' he said.

When the pig stopped squealing he leaned forward and began to pull; and very soon he hauled up a man out of the well, but the noise of some big thing swimming did not stop. It turned out from their conversation to each other, though they said little enough to me, that the second man had been hanging by one arm from the lower step of the well, the other arm being broken. The noise in the well continued, and rather puzzled me.

' "Have you got anything more down there?" ' I asked them.

' "Only a horse," ' said the one that I had mistaken for a fisherman. And he went on with his angling, until he got a pair of reins on the end of his spear. And sure enough there was a horse at the end of the reins, just as the man had said.

I admit I hadn't believed him all at once, and perhaps it is rather a lesson to us not to disbelieve a thing merely because it's unlikely; and a horse in a well seemed so very unlikely, especially a well that already had so much else in it. But I was wrong, for very soon I saw a horse's head appearing; and more than that the two men could not manage to bring to sight for a long time.'

'But what was it all about?' asked Terbut. 'What were they doing?'

'They told me that,' said Jorkens. 'They were a long while getting the horse out, and every now and then one of them would call out to me a few words of explanation: you couldn't call it a story, just explanation. And what I gathered from it all was that they had been out pig-sticking and they had come on a lot of pigs, a sounder they call them, rustling in the long grass where they could not see them. And they had ridden up to a little village and got some men to go into the grass making noises, and some of the natives had brought their dogs with them; and all the pigs had come out and they had ridden after the biggest. They got right away from the long grass at once and saw no more of it, except little patches that they scarcely noticed; in fact the one beside which we all met they never noticed at all, nor did the pig; or, if he did, he went straight for it because it reminded him of home; nor did the first horse, nor his rider. And they all went into the well.

'The pig climbed on to the horse's back, to keep himself out of the water; and the horse kept on rolling sideways as he swam, so as to put the pig back in the well. And that is another unusual thing to see, I mean a pig riding a horse; but, again, one should not disbelieve it merely on that account. I don't claim to have seen it myself, but the man who killed the pig saw it; in fact he killed it actually in the saddle. He killed the pig first because it seemed to make more room in the well, especially considering how near his tusks kept coming to the shoulder-blades of the man who was hanging by one arm from the bottom step. And then he pulled the man out. Getting the horse out was the hardest job of the lot.'

'Did you lend them a hand with the horse?' asked Terbut, rather unnecessarily.

'Well, no,' said Jorkens, 'I was perfectly ready to, but the fellow took offence at a quite natural remark that I made in all innocence. It was a simple and harmless remark, and very much to the point. But he took offence at it.'

'What did you say to him?' I asked.

'I merely said,' replied Jorkens, ' "Nice for their drinking water." '

HOW JEMBU PLAYED FOR CAMBRIDGE

The next time that Murcote brought me again to his Club we arrived a little late. Lunch was over, and nine or ten of them were gathered before that fireplace they have; and that talk of theirs had commenced, the charm of which was that there was no way of predicting upon what topics it would touch. It all depended upon who was there, and who was leading the talk, and what his mood was; and of course on all manner of irrelevant things besides, such as whiskey, and the day's news or rumour.

But to-day they had evidently all been talking of cricket, and the reason of that was clearer than men usually seem to think such reasons are. I seemed to see it almost the moment that I sat down; and nobody told it me, but the air seemed heavy with it. The reason that they talked about cricket was that there was a group there that day that were out of sympathy with Mr. Jorkens; bored perhaps by his long reminiscences, irritated by his lies, or disgusted by the untidy mess that intemperance made of his tie. Whatever it was it was clear enough that they were talking vigorously of cricket because they felt sure that that topic if well adhered to must keep the old fellow away from the trackless lands and the jungles, and that, if he must talk of Africa, it could only be to some tidy trim well-ordered civilised part of it that he could get from the subject of cricket. They felt so sure of this.

They had evidently been talking of cricket for some time, and were resolute to keep on it, when shortly after I sat down amongst them one turned to Jorkens himself and said, "Are you going to watch the match at Lord's?"

"No, no," said Jorkens sadly. "I never watch cricket now."

"But you used to a good deal, didn't you?" said another, determined not to let Jorkens get away from cricket.

"Oh yes," said Jorkens, "once; right up to that time when Cambridge beat Surrey by one run." He sighed heavily and continued: "You remember that?"

"Yes," said someone. "But tell us about it."

They thought they were on safe ground there. And so they started Jorkens upon a story, thinking they had him far from the cactus jungles. But that old wanderer was not kept so easily in English fields, his imagination to-day or his memory or whatever you call it, any more than his body had been in the old days, of which he so often told.

"It's a long story," said Jorkens. "You remember Jembu?"

"Of course," said the cricketers.

"You remember his winning hit," said Jorkens.

"Yes, a two wasn't it?" said someone.

"Yes," said Jorkens, "it was. And you remember how he got it?"

That was too much for the cricketers. None quite remembered. And then Murcote spoke. "Didn't he put it through the slips with his knee?" he said.

"Exactly," said Jorkens. "Exactly. That's what he did. Put it through the slips with his knee. And only a leg-bye. He never hit it. Only a leg-bye." And his voice dropped into mumbles.

"What did you say?" said one of the ruthless cricketers, determined to keep him to cricket.

"Only a leg-bye," said Jorkens. "He never hit it."

"Well he won the match all right," said one, "with that couple of runs. It didn't matter how he got them."

"Didn't it!" said Jorkens. "Didn't it!"

And in the silence that followed the solemnity of his emphasis he looked from face to face. Nobody had any answer. Jorkens had got them.

"I'll tell you whether it mattered or not, that couple of

leg-byes," said Jorkens then. And in the silence he told this story:

"I knew Jembu at Cambridge. He was younger than me of course, but I used to go back to Cambridge often to see those towers and the flat fen country, and so I came to know Jembu. He was no cricketer. No no, Jembu was no cricketer. He dressed as white men dress and spoke perfect English, but they could not teach him cricket. He used to play golf and things like that. And sometimes in the evening he would go right away by himself and sit down on the grass and sing. He was like that all his first year. And then one day they seem to have got him to play a bit, and then he got interested, probably because he saw the admiration they had for his marvellous fielding. But as for batting, as for making a run, well, his average was less than one in something like ten innings.

"And then he came by the ambition to play for Cambridge. You never know with these natives what on earth they will set their hearts on. And I suppose that if he had not fulfilled his ambition he would have died, or committed murder or something. But, as you know, he played for Cambridge at the end of his second year."

"Yes," said someone.

"Yes, but do you know how?" said Jorkens.

"Why by being the best bat of his time I suppose," said

Murcote.

"He never made more than fifty," said Jorkens, with a certain sly look in his eye as it seemed to me.

"No," said Murcote, "but within one or two of it whenever he went to the wickets for something like two years."

"One doesn't want more than that," said another.

"No," said Jorkens. "But he did the day that they played Surrey. Well, I'll tell you how he came to play for Cambridge."

"Yes, do," they said.

"When Jembu decided that he must play for Cambridge he practised at the nets for a fortnight, then broke his bat over his knee and disappeared."

"Where did he go to?" said someone a little incredulously.

"He went home," said Jorkens.

"Home?" they said.

"I was on the same boat with him," said Jorkens drawing himself up at the sound of doubt in their voices.

"You were going to tell us how Jembu played for Cambridge," said one called Terbut, a lawyer, who seemed as much out of sympathy with Jorkens and his ways as any of them.

"Wait a moment," said Jorkens. "I told you he could not bat. Now, when one of these African natives wants to do something that he can't, you know what he always does? He goes to a witch doctor. And when Jembu made up his mind to play for Cambridge he put the whole force of his personality into that one object, every atom of will he had inherited from all his ferocious ancestors. He gave up reading divinity, and everything, and just practised at the nets as I told you, all day long for a fortnight."

"Not an easy thing to break a bat over his knee," said Terbut.

"His strength was enormous," said Jorkens. "I was more interested in cricket in those days than in anything else. I visited Jembu in his rooms just at that time. Into the room where we sat he had put the last touches of tidiness: I never saw anything so neat, all his divinity books put away trim in their shelves, he must have had over a hundred of them, and everything in the room with that air about it that a dog would recognise as foreboding a going away.

" 'I am going home,' he said.

" 'What, giving up cricket?' I asked.

" 'No,' he answered and his gaze looked beyond me as though concerned with some far-off contentment. 'No, but I must make runs.'

" 'You want practice,' I said.

" 'I want prayer,' he answered.

" 'But you can pray here,' I said.

He shook his head.

" 'No, no,' he answered with that far-away look again.

"Well, I only cared for cricket. Nothing else interested me then. And I wanted to see how he would do it. I suppose I shouldn't trouble about it nowadays. But the memory of his perfect fielding, and his keenness for the one thing I cared about, and his tremendous ambition, as it seemed to me then, to play cricket for Cambridge, made the whole thing a quest that I must see the end of.

" 'Where will you pray?' I said.

" 'There's a man that is very good at all that sort of thing,' he answered.

" 'Where does he live?' I said.

" 'Home.'

"Well it turned out he had taken a cabin on one of the Union Castle line. And I decided to go with him. I booked my passage on the same boat; and, when we got into the Mediterranean, deck cricket began, and Jembu was always bowled in the first few balls even at that. I am no cricketer, I worshipped the great players all the more for that; I don't pretend to have been a cricketer; but I stayed at the wickets longer than Jembu every time, all through the Mediterranean till we got to the Red Sea, and it became too hot to play cricket, or even to think of it for more than a minute or two on end. The equator felt cool and refreshing after that.

And then one day we came into Killindini. Jembu had two ponies to meet us there and twenty or thirty men."

"Wired to them I suppose," said Terbut.

"No," said Jorkens. "He had wired to some sort of a missionary who was in touch with Jembu's people. Jembu you know was a pretty important chieftain, and when anyone got word to his people that Jembu wanted them, they had to come. They had tents for us, and mattresses, and they put them on their heads and carried them away through Africa, while we rode. It was before the days of the railway, and it was a long trek, and uphill all the way. We rose eight thousand feet in two hundred miles. We went on day after day into the interior of Africa: you know the country?"

"We have heard you tell of it," said someone.

"Yes, yes," said Jorkens, cutting out, as I thought, a good deal of local colour that he had intended to give us. "And one day Kenya came in sight like a head between two great shoulders; and then Jembu turned northwards. Yes, he turned northwards as far as I could make out; and travelled much more quickly; and we came to nine thousand feet, and forests of cedar. And every evening Jembu and I used to play stump cricket, and I always bowled him out in an over or two; and then the sun would set and we lit our fires."

"Was it cold?" said Terbut.

"To keep off lions," said Jorkens.

"You bowled out Jembu?" said another incredulously, urged to speech by an honest doubt, or else to turn Jorkens away from one of his interminable lion-stories.

"A hundred times," said Jorkens, "if I have done it once."

"Jembu," some of us muttered almost involuntarily, for the fame of his batting lived on, as indeed it does still.

"Wait till I tell you," said Jorkens. "In a day or two we began to leave the high ground: bamboos took the place of cedars; trees I knew nothing of took the place of bamboos; and we came in sight of hideous forests of cactus; when we burned their trunks in our camp-fires, mobs of great insects rushed out of the shrivelling bark. And one day we came in sight of hills that Jembu knew, with a forest lying dark in the valleys and folds of them, and Jembu's own honey-pots tied to the upper branches.

"These honey-pots were the principal source, I fancy, of Jembu's wealth, narrow wooden pots about three feet long, in which the wild bees lived, and guarded by men that you never see, waiting with bows and arrows. It was the harvest of these in a hundred square miles of forest that sent Jembu to Cambridge to study divinity, and learn our ways and our language. Of course he had cattle too, and plenty of ivory came his way, and raw gold now and then; and, in a quiet way, I should fancy, a good many slaves.

"Jembu's face lighted up when he saw his honey-pots, and

the forest that was his home, dark under those hills that were all flashing in sunlight. But no thought of his home or his honey-pots made him forget for a single instant his ambition to play for Cambridge, and that night at the edge of the forest he was handling a bat still, and I was still bowling him out.

"Next day we came to the huts of Jembu's people. Queer people. I should have liked to have shown you a photograph of them. I had a small camera with me. But whenever I put it up they all ran away.

"We came to their odd reed huts.

"Undergrowth had been cleared and the earth stamped hard by bare feet, but they did not ever seem to have thinned the trees, and their huts were in and out among the great trunks. My tent was set up a little way from the huts, while Jembu went to his people. Men came and offered me milk and fruit and chickens, and went away. And in the evening Jembu came to me.

" 'I am going to pray now,' he said.

"I thought he meant there and then, and rose to leave the tent to him.

" 'No,' he said, 'one can't pray by oneself.'

"Then I gathered that by 'pray' he meant some kind of worship, and that the man he had told me of in his rooms at Cambridge would be somewhere near now. I was so keen on cricket in those days that anything affecting it always seemed to me of paramount importance, and I said 'May I come too?'

"Jembu merely beckoned with his hand and walked on.

"We went through the dark of the forest for some few minutes, and saw in the shade a great building standing alone. A sort of cathedral of thatch. Inside, a great space seemed bare. The walls near to the ground were of reed and ivory: above, it was all a darkness of rafters and thatch. The long thin reeds were vertical, and every foot or so a great tusk of an elephant stood upright in the wall. Nuggets of gold here and there were fastened against the tusks by thin strands of copper. Presently I could make out that a thin line of brushwood was laid in a wide circle on the floor. Inside it Jembu sat down on the hard mud. And I went far away from it and sat in a corner, though not too near to the reeds, because, if anything would make a good home for a cobra, they would. And Jembu said never a word; and I waited.

"Then a man stepped through the reeds in the wall that Jembu was facing, dressed in a girdle of feathers hanging down from his loins, wing feathers they seemed to be, out of a crane. He went to some sort of iron pot that stood on the floor, that I had not noticed before, and lifted the lid and took fire from it, and lit the thin line of brushwood that ran round Jembu. Then he began to dance. He must have been twelve or fifteen feet from Jembu when he began to dance, and he danced round him in circles, or leapt is a better word, for it was too fierce for a dance. He took no notice of me. After he had been dancing some time I saw that his circles were narrowing; and presently he came to the line of brushwood at a point that the fire had not reached, and leapt through it and danced on round Jembu. Jembu sat perfectly still, with his eyes fixed. The weirdest shadows were galloping now round the walls from the waving flames of the brushwood; and any man such as us must have been sick and giddy from the frightful pace of those now narrow circles that he was making round Jembu, but he leapt nimbly on. He was within a few feet of my friend now. What would he do, I was wondering, when he reached him? Still Jembu never stirred, either hand or eyelid. Stray leaves drifting up from the dancing savage's feet were already settling on Jembu. And all of a sudden the black dancer fainted.

"He lay on the ground before Jembu, his feet a yard from him, and one arm flung out away from him, so that that hand lay in the brushwood. The flames were near to the hand, but Jembu never stirred. They reached it and scorched it: Jembu never lifted a finger, and the heathen dancer neither moved nor flinched. I knew then that this swoon that he had gone into was a real swoon, whatever was happening. The flames died down round the hand, died down round the whole circle; till only a glow remained, and the shadow of Jembu was as still on the wall as a black bronze image of Buddha.

"I began to get up then, with the idea of doing something for the unconscious man, but Jembu caught the movement, slight as it was, although he was not looking at me; and, still without giving me a glance of his eye, waved me sharply away with a jerk of his left hand. So I left the man lying there, as silent as Jembu. And there I sat, while Jembu seemed not to be breathing, and the embers went out and the place seemed dimmer than ever for the light of the fire that was gone. And then the dancing man came to, and got up and bent over Jembu, and spoke to him, and turned; and all at once he was gone through the slit in the reeds by which he had entered the temple. Then Jembu turned his head, and I looked at him.

" 'He has promised,' he said.

" 'Who?' I asked.

" 'Mungo,' said Jembu.

" 'Was that Mungo?' I asked.

" 'He? No! Only his servant.'

" 'Who is Mungo?' I asked.

" 'We don't know,' said Jembu, with so much finality that I said no more of that.

"But I asked what he had promised.

" 'Fifty runs,' replied Jembu.

" 'In one innings?' I asked.

" 'Whenever I bat,' said Jembu.

" 'Whenever you bat!' I said. 'Why! That will get you into any eleven. Once or twice would attract notice, but a steady average of fifty, and always to be relied on, it mayn't be spectacular, but you'd be the prop of any eleven.'

"He seemed so sure of it that I was quite excited; I could not imagine a more valuable man to have in a team than one who could always do that, day after day, against any kind of bowling, on a good wicket or bad.

" 'But I must never make more,' said Jembu.

" 'You'll hardly want to,' I said.

" 'Not a run more,' said Jembu, gazing straight at the wall.

" 'What will happen if you do?' I asked.

" 'You never know with Mungo,' Jembu replied.

" 'Don't you?' I said.

" 'No man knows that,' said Jembu.

" 'You'll be able to play for Cambridge now,' I said.

"Jembu got up from the floor and we came away.

"He spoke to his people that evening in the firelight. Told them he was going back to Cambridge again, told them what he was going to do there, I suppose; though what they made of it, or what they thought Cambridge was, Mungo only knows. But I saw from his face, and from theirs, that he made that higher civilisation, to which he was going back, very beautiful to them, a sort of landmark far far on ahead of them, to which I suppose they thought that they would one day come themselves. Fancy them playing cricket!

"Well, next day we turned round and started back again, hundreds of miles to the sea. The lions. . ."

"We've heard about them," said Terbut.

"Oh well," said Jorkens.

But if they wouldn't hear his lion-stories they wanted to hear how Jembu played for Cambridge: it was the glamour of Jembu's name after all these years that was holding them. And soon he was back with his story of the long trek to the sea from somewhere North of a line between Kenya and the great lake.

He told us of birds that to me seemed quite incredible, birds with horny faces, and voices like organ-notes; and he told us of the cactus-forests again, speaking of cactus as though it could grow to the size of trees; and he told us of the falls of the Guaso Nyero, going down past a forest trailing grey beards of moss; there may be such falls as he told of above some such forest, but we thought more likely he had picked up tales of some queer foreign paradise, and was giving us them as geography, or else that he had smoked opium or some such drug, and had dreamed of them. One never knew with Jorkens.

He told us how they came to the coast again; and apparently there are trees in Mombasa with enormous scarlet flowers, that I have often seen made out of linen in windows of drapers' shops, but according to him they are real.

Well, I will let him tell his own story.

"We had to wait in that oven" (he meant Mombasa) "for several days before we could get a ship, and when we got home the cricket season was over. It was an odd thing, but Jembu went to the nets at once, and began hitting about, as he had been doing in the Red Sea; and there was no doubt about it that he was an unmistakable batsman. And he always stopped before there was any possibility that he could by any means be supposed to have made fifty.

"I talked to him about Mungo now and then but could get nothing much out of him: he became too serious for that, whenever one mentioned Mungo, and of the dancing man in the temple I got barely a word; indeed I never even knew his name. He read divinity still, but not with the old zest, so far as I could gather whenever I went to see him, and I think that his thoughts were far away with Mungo.

"And as soon as May came round he was back at cricket; and sure enough, as you know, he played for Cambridge. That was the year he played first; and you have only to look at old score books to see that he never made less than forty-six all that year. He always got very shy when he neared fifty:

he was too afraid of a four if he passed forty-six, and that was why he always approached it so gingerly, often stopping at forty-seven, though what he liked to do was to get to forty-six and then to hit a four and hear them applauding his fifty. For he was very fond of the good opinion of Englishmen, though the whole of our civilisation was really as nothing to him, compared with the fear of Mungo.

"Well, his average was magnificent; considering how often he was not out, it must have been nearly eighty. And then next year was the year he played against Surrey. All through May and June he went on with his forty-seven, forty-eight, forty-nine and fifty; and Cambridge played Surrey early in July. I needn't tell you of that match; after Oxford v. Cambridge in 1870, and Eton v. Harrow in 1910, I suppose it's the best-remembered match in history. You remember how Cambridge had two runs to win and Jembu was in with Halket, the last wicket. Halket was their wicket-keeper and hardly able to deal with this situation; at least Jembu thought not, for he had obviously been getting the bowling all to himself for some time. But now he had made fifty. With the whole ground roaring applause at Jembu's fifty, and two runs still to win I laid a pretty large bet at two to one against Cambridge. Most of them knew his peculiarity of not passing fifty, but I was the only man on the ground that knew of his fear of Mungo. I alone had seen his face when the dancing man went round him, I alone knew the terms. The bet was a good deal more than I could afford. A good deal more. Well, Jembu had the bowling, two to win, and the first ball he stopped very carefully; and then one came a little outside the off stump; and Jembu put his leg across the wicket and played the ball neatly through the slips with his knee. They ran two, and the game was over. Jembu's score of course stayed at fifty, no leg-byes could affect that, as anyone knows who has ever heard of cricket. How could anyone think otherwise? But that damned African spirit knew nothing of cricket. How should he know, if you come to think of it? Born probably ages ago in some tropical marsh, from which he had risen to hang over African villages, haunting old women and travellers lost in the forest, or blessing or cursing the crops with moods that changed with each wind, what should he know of the feelings or rules of a sportsman? Spirits like that keep their word as far as I've known: it was nothing but honest ignorance; and he had credited poor Jembu with fifty-two though not a ball that had touched his bat that day had had any share in more than fifty runs.

"And I've learned this of life, that you must abide by the mistakes of your superiors. Your own you may sometimes atone for, but with the mistakes of your superiors, so far as they affect you, there is nothing to do but to suffer for them.

"There was no appeal for Jembu against Mungo's mistake. Who would have listened to him? Certainly no one here: certainly no one in Africa. Jembu went back to see what Mungo had done, as soon as he found out the view that Mungo had taken. He found out that soon enough, by dropping back to his old score of one and nothing in three consecutive innings. The Cambridge captain assured him that that might happen to anybody, and that he mustn't think of giving up cricket. But Jembu knew. And he went back to his forest beyond Mount Kenya, to see what Mungo had done.

"And only a few years later I came on Jembu again, in a small hotel in Marseilles, where they give you excellent fish. They have them in a little tank of water, swimming about alive, and you choose your fish and they cook it. I went there only three or four years after that match against Surrey, being in Marseilles for a day; and a black waiter led me to the glass tank, and I looked up from the fishes, and it was Jembu. And we had a long talk, and he told me all that had happened because of those two leg-byes that had never been near his bat.

"It seems that a tribe that had never liked Jembu's people had broken into his forest and raided his honey-pots. They had taken his ivory, and burnt his cathedral of thatch, and driven off all his slaves. I knew from speeches that he had made at Cambridge that Jembu in principle was entirely opposed to slavery; but it is altogether another matter to have one's slaves driven away, and not know where they have gone to or whether they will be well cared for. It was that that broke his heart as much as the loss of his honey-pots; and they got his wives too. His people were scattered, and all his cattle gone; there was nothing after that raid left for Jembu in Africa.

"He wandered down to the coast; he tried many jobs; but Mungo was always against him. He drifted to Port Said as a stowaway, to Marseilles as a sailor, and there deserted, and was many things more, before he rose to the position of waiter; and I question if Mungo had even done with him then. A certain fatalistic feeling he had, which he called resignation, seemed to bear him up and to comfort him. The word resignation, I think, came out of his books of divinity; but the feeling came from far back, out of old dark forests of Africa. And, wherever it came from, it cheered him awhile at his work in that inn of Marseilles, and caused him to leave gravy just where it fell, on the starched shirt-front that he wore all day. He was not unhappy, but he looked for nothing better; after all, he had won that match for Cambridge against Surrey, I don't see what more he could want, and many a man has less. But when I said good-bye to him I felt sure that Mungo would never alter his mind, either to understand, or to pardon, those two leg-byes."

"Did you ask him," said Terbut, "how Mungo knew that he got those two leg-byes?"

"No," said Jorkens, "I didn't ask him that."

THE FIELD WHERE THE SATYRS DANCED

There is a field above my house in which I sometimes walk in the evening. And whenever I go there in summer I always see the same thing, very small and far off, the tiniest fraction of the wide view that one has, and not appearing until one has looked for it a little carefully – a field surrounded by woods, a green space all among shadows, which suggested to me, the very first time I saw it, an odd idea. But the idea was so evanescent, and floated by so like a travelling butterfly, that by the time I went again a few days later to look at the view at evening I barely remembered it. But then the idea came again, coming as suddenly as a wind that got up soon after sunset, bringing the chill of night a little before its time. And the idea was that to that field at evening satyrs slipped out of the woods to dance on the grass.

This time I did not forget the idea at all; on the contrary it rather haunted me, but down in the valley it grew to seem so unlikely that one put it away as one puts away lumber of old collections, scarcely counting it any more, though knowing that it was there.

And then one evening, the nightingale's song being over for many days, and hay ripening, it struck me that if I wanted to see the wild roses I must go soon or they would all be over, and I should have to wait another year to see what we can only see for a limited number of times; so I went up the field again behind my house, on the hill. It is a perfectly ordinary field, even though at one end the hedge has run a bit wild and is one bank of wild roses. I do not know why one calls it an ordinary field, nor why one sometimes feels of another field that it lies deep under enchantment, yet ordinary it was; one felt sure of that as one walked in it.

On my way to the wild roses at the far end of the field, with my back to the view of the valley, I almost felt as though something behind me and far away were beckoning. For a moment I felt it and the feeling passed, and I walked on toward the wild roses. Then it came again, and I turned round to look; and there was the view over the valley the same as it ever looked, rather featureless from the loss of the sunlight and not yet mysterious with night. I moved my eyes left-handed along the far ridge. And soon they fell on the field where the satyrs danced. Of this I was certain: they danced there. Nothing had changed in the view; the far field was the same as ever, a little mysterious around its edges and flat and green in the middle, high up on the top of a hill; but the certainty had grown and become immense. It was just too far to see if anything moved in the shadows, too far to see if anything came from the wood, but I was sure that this was a dancing ground of those that lurked in the dark of the distant trees, and that they were satyrs. And all things darkened towards the likely hour, till the field was too dim to see at that great distance, and I went home down the hill. And that night and all the next day the certainty remained with me, so that I decided that evening to go to the field and see.

The field where the satyrs danced was some way from my house, so I started a while before sunset, and climbed the far hill in the cool. There I came by a little road scarce more than a lane that ran deep through a wood of Spanish chestnut and oak, to a great road of tar.

Down this I walked for a bit while the twentieth century streamed by me, with its machinery, its crowds, and its speed; flowing from urban sources. It was as though for a while I waded in a main current of time. But soon I saw a lane on the other side of it that ran in what should be the direction of my field; and I crossed the road of tar, and soon I was in a rural quiet again that time seemed scarcely to bother about. And so I came to the woods that I knew surrounded the field. Hazel and oak they were and masses of dogwood, on the right, and on the left they were thinning down to a hedge; and over the hedge I suddenly saw the field.

Ahead of me, on the far side of the field, the wood was dense and old. On my right lay, as I have said, oak, hazel, and dogwood; and on the left, where the field dipped down to the valley, I saw the tops of old oaks. It was an idyllic scene amongst all that circle of woods. All the more so by contrast with the road of tar. But the moment I looked at the field I realised that there was nothing unearthly about it. There were a few buttercups growing in a very sparse crop of hay; dog daisies farther off and patches of dry brown earth showing through, and unmistakably over the whole field an ordinary air of everyday. Whatever there is in enchantment is hard to define, or whatever magic is visible from the touch of fabulous things, but amongst these buttercups and dog daisies and poor crop of hay it certainly was not.

I looked up from the field over the tops of the oaks that grew on the slope of the valley, to be sure by looking across that I had come to the right field. If I could see, and only just see, the field of the wild roses, then this field and these woods must be the ones that I sought. And sure enough, I saw the unmistakable hills from which I had come, and the woods along the top of them, and above these woods a field. For a moment I could not be sure. So strange it looked, so haunted – not by shadows, for the sun was long set, but by a certain darkness gathering under the hedges while the gloaming still shone on its centre – that I did not immediately know it. And, as I watched it and recognised it by many landmarks as my very ordinary field, the mystery deepened and deepened, until before the gloaming faded away it was obviously touched by that eeriness that is never found far from the haunt of fabulous things.

It was too far to get there tonight, and I looked once more at the field by whose edges I stood, to see if anything lurked at all of the magic that it had had. No, nothing; it was all gone. At this moment a rustic boy skipped out of the wood and came over the field towards me. And something about him made him seem so much at home in that field and so knowing of all its neighbouring shrubs and shadows that, clinging still to a last vestige of my fancy, I hailed him, and he pricked up his ears. Then I asked, just as I might have asked if the buses were running: 'Do the satyrs dance here tonight?'

'Here? NO!' he said with such certainty that I knew for sure I was wrong.

I mumbled something like that I thought they were going to.

'No,' he said, shaking his head and pointing away to my field of the wild roses, gleaming only faintly now, a dim grey-green before nightfall, 'they are dancing there tonight.'

THE BUREAU D'ECHANGE DE MAUX

I often think of the Bureau d'Echange de Maux and the wondrously evil old man that sat therein. It stood in a little street that there is in Paris, its doorway made of three brown beams of wood, the top one overlapping the others like the Greek letter *pai*, all the rest painted green, a house far lower and narrower than its neighbours and infinitely stranger, a thing to take one's fancy. And over the doorway on the old brown beam in faded yellow letters this legend ran, 'Bureau Universel d'Echange de Maux'.

I entered at once and accosted the listless man that lolled on a stool by his counter. I demanded the wherefore of his wonderful house, what evil wares he exchanged, with many other things that I wished to know, for curiosity led me: and indeed had it not I had gone at once from the shop, for there was so evil a look in that fattened man, in the hang of his fallen cheeks and his sinful eye, that you would have said he had had dealings with Hell and won the advantage by sheer wickedness.

Such a man was mine host, but above all the evil of him lay in his eyes, which lay so still, so apathetic, that you would have sworn that he was drugged or dead; like lizards motionless on a wall they lay, then suddenly they darted, and all his cunning flamed up and revealed itself in what one

74

moment before seemed no more than a sleepy and ordinary wicked old man. And this was the object and trade of that peculiar shop, the Bureau Universel d'Echange de Maux: you paid twenty francs, which the old man proceeded to take from me, for admission to the bureau, and then had the right to exchange any evil or misfortune with anyone on the premises for some evil or misfortune that he 'could afford', as the old man put it.

There were four or five men in the dingy ends of that low-ceilinged room who gesticulated and muttered softly in twos as men who make a bargain, and now and then more came in, and the eyes of the flabby owner of the house leaped up at them as they entered, seemed to know their errands at once and each one's peculiar need, and fell back again into somnolence, receiving his twenty francs in an almost lifeless hand and biting the coin as though in pure absence of mind.

'Some of my clients,' he told me. So amazing to me was the trade of this extraordinary shop that I engaged the old man in conversation, repulsive though he was, and from his garrulity I gathered these facts. He spoke in perfect English though his utterance was somewhat thick and heavy, no language seemed to come amiss to him. He had been in business a great many years, how many he would not say, and was far older than he looked. All kinds of people did business in his shop. What they exchanged with each other he did not care, except that it had to be evils; he was not empowered to carry on any other kind of business.

There was no evil, he told me, that was not negotiable there; no evil the old man knew had ever been taken away in despair from his shop. A man might have to wait and come back again next day and next day and the day after, paying twenty francs each time, but the old man had the addresses of his clients and shrewdly knew their needs, and soon the right two met and eagerly changed their commodities. 'Commodities' was the old man's terrible word, said with a gruesome smack of his heavy lips, for he took a pride in his business and evils to him were goods.

I learned from him in ten minutes very much of human nature, more than I had ever learned from any other man; I learned from him that a man's own evil is to him the worst thing that there is or could be, and that an evil so unbalances all men's minds that they always seek for extremes in that small grim shop. A woman that had no children had exchanged with an impoverished half-maddened creature with twelve. On one occasion a man had exchanged wisdom for folly.

'Why on earth did he do that?' I said.

'None of my business,' the old man answered in his heavy indolent way. He merely took his twenty francs from each and ratified the agreement in the little room at the back opening out of the shop where his clients do business. Apparently the man that had parted with wisdom had left the shop upon the tips of his toes with a happy though foolish expression all over his face, but the other went thoughtfully away wearing a troubled and very puzzled look. Almost always it seemed they did business in opposite evils.

But the thing that puzzled me most in all my talks with that unwieldy man, the thing that puzzles me still, is that none that had once done business in that shop ever returned again; a man might come day after day for many weeks, but once do business and he never returned; so much the old man told me, but, when I asked him why, he only muttered that he did not know.

It was to discover the wherefore of this strange thing, and for no other reason at all, that I determined myself to do business sooner or later in the little room at the back of that mysterious shop. I determined to exchange some very trivial evil for some evil equally slight, to seek for myself an advantage so very small as scarcely to give Fate as it were a grip; for I deeply distrusted these bargains, knowing well that man has never yet benefited by the marvellous and that the more miraculous his advantage appears to be the more securely and tightly do the gods or the witches catch him. In a few days more I was going back to England and I was beginning to fear that I should be sea-sick: this fear of sea-sickness, not the actual malady but only the mere fear of it, I decided to exchange for a suitably little evil. I did not know with whom I should be dealing, who in reality was the head of the firm (one never does when shopping), but I decided that neither Jew nor Devil could make very much on so small a bargain as that.

I told the old man my project, and he scoffed at the smallness of my commodity, trying to urge me on to some darker bargain, but could not move me from my purpose. And then he told me tales with a somewhat boastful air of the big business, the great bargains, that had passed through his hands. A man had once run in there to try and exchange death; he had swallowed poison by accident and had only twelve hours to live. That sinister old man had been able to oblige him. A client was willing to exchange the commodity.

'But what did he give in exchange for death?' I said.

'Life,' said that grim old man with a furtive chuckle.

'It must have been a horrible life,' I said.

'That was not my affair,' the proprietor said, lazily rattling together as he spoke a little pocketful of twenty-franc pieces.

Strange business I watched in that shop for the next few days, the exchange of odd commodities, and heard strange mutterings in corners amongst couples who presently rose and went to the back room, the old man following to ratify.

Twice a day for a week I paid my twenty francs, watching life with its great needs and its little needs morning and afternoon spread out before me in all its wonderful variety.

And one day I met a comfortable man with only a little need, he seemed to have the very evil I wanted. He always feared the lift was going to break. I knew too much of hydraulics to fear things as silly as that, but it was not my business to cure his ridiculous fear. Very few words were needed to convince him that mine was the evil for him, he never crossed the sea, and I, on the other hand, could always walk upstairs, and I also felt at the time, as many must feel in that shop, that so absurd a fear could never trouble me. And yet at times it is almost the curse of my life. When we both had signed the parchment in the spidery back room and the old man had signed and ratified (for which we had to pay him fifty francs each) I went back to my hotel, and there I saw the deadly thing in the basement. They asked me if I would go upstairs in the lift; from force of habit I risked it, and I held my breath all the way up and clenched my hands. Nothing will induce me to try such a journey again. I would sooner go up to my room in a balloon. And why? Because if a balloon goes wrong you have a chance, it may spread out into a parachute after it has burst, it may catch in a tree, a hundred and one things may happen, but if the lift falls down its shaft you are done. As for sea-sickness I shall never be sick again, I cannot tell you why except that I know that it is so.

And the shop in which I made this remarkable bargain, the shop to which none return when their business is done: I set out for it next day. Blindfold I could have found my way to the unfashionable quarter out of which a mean street runs, where you take the alley at the end, whence runs the cul-de-sac where the queer shop stood. A shop with pillars, fluted and painted red, stands on its near side, its other neighbour is a low-class jeweller's with little silver brooches in the window. In such incongruous company stood the shop with beams, with its walls painted green.

In half an hour I stood in the cul-de-sac to which I had gone twice a day for the last week. I found the shop with the ugly painted pillars and the jeweller that sold brooches, but the green house with the three beams was gone.

Pulled down, you will say, although in a single night. That can never be the answer to the mystery, for the house of the fluted pillars painted on plaster, and the low-class jeweller's shop with its silver brooches (all of which I could identify one by one) were standing side by side.